Catwalk
and Overpass

By the same author:

THE PUNISHED LAND   1980

HOLD FAST   1985

FOURTEEN ISRAELI POETS:
A SELECTION OF MODERN HEBREW POETRY
(together with Harold Schimmel)

RETRIEVEMENTS: A JERUSALEM ANTHOLOGY

poems by
Dennis Silk

CATWALK
and OVERPASS

Viking

VIKING
Published by the Penguin Group
Viking Penguin, a division of Penguin Books USA Inc.,
375 Hudson Street, New York, New York 10014, U.S.A.
Penguin Books Ltd, 27 Wrights Lane,
London W8 5TZ, England
Penguin Books Australia Ltd, Ringwood,
Victoria, Australia
Penguin Books Canada Ltd, 2801 John Street,
Markham, Ontario, Canada L3R 1B4
Penguin Books (N.Z.) Ltd, 182–190 Wairau Road,
Auckland 10, New Zealand

Penguin Books Ltd, Registered Offices:
Harmondsworth, Middlesex, England

First published in 1990 by Viking Penguin,
a division of Penguin Books USA Inc.

10 9 8 7 6 5 4 3 2 1

Different versions of the "Stingy Kids" sequence
appeared in Grand Street, The Jerusalem Post, and
The Tel Aviv Review. "Truant" was previously published
in Shenandoah; "In Memoriam" in The American Voice;
"1948" in Retrievements; and "Eating Out" in Stand.
Mr. Silk's translation of "Dream Canaan" by
Aba Stolzenberg first appeared in The Penguin Book
of Modern Yiddish Verse edited by Irving Howe,
Ruth R. Wisse, and Khone Shmeruk, published by
Viking Penguin, Copyright © Irving Howe,
Ruth Wisse, and Khone Shmeruk, 1987.

LIBRARY OF CONGRESS CATALOGING IN PUBLICATION DATA
Silk, Dennis, 1928–
Catwalk and overpass : poems/Dennis Silk.
p. cm.
ISBN 0-670-82781-9
I. Title.
PR9510.9.S57C3 1990   89-40595
821—dc20

Printed in the United States of America
Set in Bembo
Designed by Liney Li

For Ziva Caspi

"And first to know thine own state, then the State's."

—*Ben Jonson*

Contents

CATWALK AND OVERPASS

LANDING	3
YAH!	4
THOMPSON STREET	6
SEASIDE	8
THE WAY	9
TELL-TALE	10
CAIRO JUSTICE	11
THE CLOUD IN CAIRO	12
THE BALANCE	13
LOCATION	15

ARGUMENT   21
PUBLIC TRANSPORT   23
"THE MOONLIGHT PROPHET FELT THE MADDING
   HOUR"   24
NEOLOGISM   25
ON THE SITUATION   26
ODD MAN   27
COUTURIER   28
DREAM-TIME   29
FLOWN IN   30
TRUANTS   31
ON THE WAY TO THE TERRITORIES   32
STINGY DUNAMS   33
NOT SETTLING BUT SHUTTLING   34
ZAP AND THE CAP'N   35
   ACE   35
   EGGWARDS   36
   THREE SILLY STRATEGISTS   39
NARK'S HOLIDAY   41
VANISHING TRICK   42
WRECKERS   43
ON THE HOUSETOPS OF BALATA   44
NOBLE ENCLOSURE   45
BLOWING IT UP   47
GAUDY EVENING UNDER MOUNT SION   48
AMBUSH   49
ARMOURY   50
INDEPENDENCE DAY 1987   51
AMATEUR   52
PASTORAL   53
SEA MILES   54

WATERING PLACE   55
RAFT   56
THE RELIEF   57
AFTER THE WAR   58
Notes for STINGY KIDS   59

WOYZECK

WOYZECK   63
THE DOCTOR   64

A CLOUD INHALED ME

TRUANT   67
CASUALTY   68
BREACH   69
A CLOUD INHALED ME   70

HERE IS THE ALBUM OF PALESTINE

DREAM CANAAN   73
AMONG THE SAMARITANS   75
THE HOLY FIRE   78
THE BOATWOMAN   80
IN MEMORIAM   82
BOOK OF HOURS   84
JAFFA GATE   85
A MISUNDERSTANDING   86
DO IT YOURSELF   88
PERFORMANCES   89
1948   90
CHRISTMAS   91

EATING OUT

EATING OUT   95
THINKING ABOUT GABRIEL   96
LUCKY STRIKE   97
AERIAL DAYS   98
UPTOWN   99
MILLAMANT TO MIRABELL   100

Catwalk and Overpass

≡ LANDING

A key-ring and the gridded floor
of this town.
            I am free
of several households as a man is free
who is numbered at every intersection.

The flashing names and faces
that smile and ask to be accounted
and jostle and allow such freedoms
as I may take—
I run toward them to avoid
such heaped plates.

I am in a cell
of the huge town, have escaped
the others I wincing ran toward
there, that other town
that liked me, also.
                        Many towns
tire.

It is between towns
I like best or, slantwise to the grid,
to have the courage of a left hand
snatching away the right's handshake.

3 / Dennis · Silk

☰ YAH!

Perhaps you will sit with me inside this insult
I till so patiently.

You found this space by leaping into it
with splayed fingers and *Yah*—
yes you did—
sharp blur of a reeky fire
makes it hard to say how big it is
but it is big.

Scared of stretch space crams itself
with catwalks of conjecture:

You did that with your hand.
Did you do that?
Did the children, with plasticine,
make a paradise of their quarrel?

Catwalk.

I maintain this freak of iron
and conduct myself to the end of the walk.

Toppling learnedly because
thinking about you I did not watch out,
I allow myself this upside-down
wait in the safety-net of the vacuum.

Let me conduct you to your catwalk.
Don't falter.

For I am your pretend-friend
and plant and water in you
a notion that cannot fruit
in the filled-in blank you advance into.

Here is one going nowhere
that rams yours amidship,
then we spill down
into the insult-space that holds us.

Yah as we somersault.

≡ THOMPSON STREET

Why, it is quarter of ten
on Thompson, quite late I wake who was early.

A blurring machine
worked in my night.
If I open the blind
it will be light of dots.

Thompson, where I paddle,
is all right, almost. Merkaya—
her name retrieves a Polynesian grandmother
though she seems Californian straightforward—
rented me this chance.
I paddle around here.

Thompson—oddly, I think of boots
and direction—
is an unforthright locus.
At my intersection
four streets wipe each other out.
They outdanced the grid
and this is what happened.

Pell-mell clogs.

It is hard to spruce up these streets.

I'd need all day on the overpass.

If a fumbler in street-maps
could locate the blur—
if *if* tilted toward him
and *through* went up to pass over—
not on the useless errand of a catwalk
giddying to run—

he'd have a hat, a mac, a learned brow,
all day, on an overpass
civic and pleading to be used.

SEASIDE

Catwalk of a pier with peeled planks
Saturday people
don't use any more but walk
under its no floor and stare through
at a Woyzeck moon thinking planning something for Marie.

☰ THE WAY

You ask about my time in Egypt.

A praying mantis and a filthy cat
point the way.
It is hopeless and so I follow it.
I am your mendicant.

Mantis for orientation.

There's a slap looking for your face
and I am your mendicant.

Slapping faces in a vacuum
is not an occupation.

A cat looks over its shoulder
at my mistake.

I.

Who said the heart—that tell-tale, and what a tale—isn't trash?

Temple area covered with shit by its conqueror. Colluding. Who'd clean it up, throw a first pailful into the wadi?

I I.

Whose tooth? His began, mine took over. He said me a name, I say it back. A tooth for a Tartuffe. That's for you, shitmonger.

CAIRO JUSTICE

Thoth and Anubis: Kate Greenaway creatures but awry. Saying, 'You've not been nice to thankworthy women.'

'Not nice to me, either,' I'm saying. Not more than forty-five percent nice.

'Another forty-five percenter,' Thoth is saying. So we make up the accounts all night.

THE CLOUD IN CAIRO

It is the dun worry—
a many-windowed clerk
at his displacement of files—
or I brought its brother:
my account-keeping cloud,
touchy as I know how to be,
and trouble-maker.

Anyway, this thriving family-concern
clouds the overpasses of the Cairenes,
and dust honks . . . I'll spit it out
and acquit myself.

Spit out Egypt?

No but this actuarial sound that clogs.

Shall a cloud inhale us?

Sons of Horus, let us flounder toward
insouciant handclaps among dust.

THE BALANCE

I was ushered into the town by Abu Tnuot—Father of
Gestures—the hotel commissionaire, and each gesture's
worth the pourboire of a Texan. He told me to spend
sleepless nights, and sink through pavements of remorse.
He said, *They're waiting for you at Tahrir.*

You drift there with dust in your teeth but the Nile's your
spittoon. A posse of gods was waiting for me at Tahrir.
My bad conscience in Cairo chooses this formal shape.
Horus and Anubis berate me. I need them to consolidate
my vapours. No one knows where the Judgement Hall is
but I do. Ibis Thoth jots down my sentence. Here it's
decided in the street. Spiteful superior creatures and they
won't let me get to the overpass. (Hundreds of people use
it, thereby avoiding such grime.) Security force people but
I know them. Berated in Tahrir, place of grime and over-
reach. What I did elsewhere—what hysteria fright jealousy
compounded in another town—they measure on their Bal-
ance of six thousand years. Jaywalker Cairenes look on as
the dusty feather of my truth testifies against me. The
devourer of the dead ponders whether to convert crouch
into pounce. She's hard to sort out—lioness with hippo
backparts but some other animal's snout. I'm not sure what
she is but it's her rôle to eat.

The meal shifts from town to town. A thrilling musical gamut occupied and devoured me. Women I'd thought colleagues in a lucid enterprise. They stood in a right way and sang. I'd thought all things musical. A chair had its right note, a boot brush, a hat. We'd contrived together a musical theatre that gave back the world-furniture to God. Unluckily, these virtuous sirens turned into screech owls and flapped spite in my eyes. For I was the angry though scared man.

The elegist for his theatre shifts the blame from town to town. Here's a catwalk of conjecture for a lifetime. (Later, this force will disperse, around the aimless but well-guarded town, and talk my case over at an embassy door or outside some prominent building.)

☰ LOCATION

A sneaky helicopter backs off but lands
vapourish young men.

They raise a night-stick in Virginia.

Above this lawn labelled CALM
backs off lands but
backs off.

Do they think they are in Palestine?
It is another lost troop.

Many.

They drift to Chicago
and wake up in Cairo.

Many
towns tire.

Paleginia?

Nettalin
wanes and re-forms.

Netta lin.

If I could locate the blur
I would be with her.

Nettalin and again
Nettalin
walks with Mayaan, opens her
coat
for him to be safe under.

Not a son of dots.
                      An
ubis

judges the useless
and again the useless,
on the catwalk,
in Cairo,
errand of a night-stick.

Heartsmiths
assay grime.

Nettalin
washes from his face fear
at the overpass.

Ann taught me
to tie her shoe, pointed doctrine, drives,
quick girl, braking, slow,
to the cavern at Shenandoah.

And again Ann and
again an
eyelash and a red
at blue ridge a red
eyelash.

From Shenandoah to NY 400 miles.

10 seeds of night-blooming vine
Ann left
I am to plant in
Virusalem?

If I could locate the blur
I'd plant them everywhere.

Linked, toward the overpass,
a kind of extended family
of night *N*s,
an upward homing
loop.

An
ubis pities
boomerang of the night-stick
and timid catwalk extension
of the foot.

And again these
and again these
seeds of night-stuff

on a long Virginian loop

                              that did
                              outdance the grid.

Stingy Kids

" 'E ate my cakes, 'e 'ad my booze,
And then 'e went 'ome to 'is mother to snooze.
Stingy kid!"

—*Lancashire traditional*

Argument. A cartographer does his variations on an antique illustrated map of Palestine. Instead of a sheik pointing a spear from Arabia Deserta, an armed enthusiast from the Jewish enclave at Hebron. On the Mount of Olives he touches in, waving a Kalachnikov and calipers, a millenarian hatching his plan for the Third Temple.

Israel is densely sown with these types. The braggart soldier, and his buttressing lawyer friend, gesture to us from the Territories. These stock types, these simplified humours, aren't marginal but straddle the map. Yet they've a skinny sense of the situation. They don't know patriotism must be bifocal. Israel—Palestine—first cousins. They don't want to focus. They've a self-sufficiency fed by a morose and inturned culture. Their posture is a stingy one: hands pushing away, averted head and heart. Hell enough!

Anger does not recommend. Then perhaps the banter of the old English poets and wits can help. They met their times—persecution, civil war, entire suburbs of dunces—

with "intellectual gaiety". So I enlist George Etherege, nonchalant Restoration wit, to dawdle with me through *The Book of Joshua*. Alexander Pope provides the coordinates to pinpoint "the Moonlight Prophet", Rabbi L★★★, at Silwan.

≡ PUBLIC TRANSPORT

There are today in Aleppo twenty prophets,
among them Rabbi Galante and Master Aaron
Isaiah ha-Kohen, and four prophetesses.

—LETTER QUOTED IN GERSHOM SCHOLEM'S *SABBATAI SEVI*

Number Sixty Two bus-stop outside Tzavta, for instance.
Sixty Two, a thick number, transports you to the morose
town of Hebron.

Zeal-of-the-Land Busy and Win-the-Fight Littlewit stand
here with briefcases of important documents. Vague
though powerful waves thud about them. You sniff the
smoke of the Third Temple.

Someone mad as they drives up to rescue them from mere
town. He retrieves them for Hebron. Zeal-of-the-Land
Busy and Win-the-Fight Littlewit descend into the bus of
a school of prophets, an artillery spotter, several sacrificial
doves and a deranged map-reader.

≡ "THE MOONLIGHT PROPHET
≡ FELT THE MADDING HOUR"

Why, that must be Rabbi L★★★. In a mucksweat under the east wall of Jerusalem. This temple-plotter looks up at much more than a finger of moon over town. A local infection spreads. He howls because he's moon-mad. With the shove he gets from up there he lopes back to Hebron.

Generosity shrinks as he lopes. The fig trees of Silwan say: *Stingy kid.*

His midwife helpmeet waits with cold wet towels for a steamy forehead. She says, 'It's all right, all right.' Madam Mandrake yanks out his howls. The ungenerous litter of his thoughts bark, all night, and wake up anyone needing a decent night's sleep, in the town of Hebron.

NEOLOGISM

I'm in my friend's garden in Abu Tor, numbering the
streaks in a tulip, when the new species draws up. Straight
from the Gehenna nursery. We spot a man with an As-
syrian beard and competent movements. Field-glasses to
his eyes, through the car window, a tactician appraises
Mount Sion's arid slope. Then off, in mufti, with the dis-
patch of a temple-plotter. It's a hybrid in motion, it's a
militarabbi.

How they wept because they hadn't carried out God's will, which was (according to the Joshua scribe) to be nasty. They called the place *Bechi*—that is, Weeping. I need the dangerous banter of Etherege to save me in *The Book of Joshua*.

When they blew up the mayors' cars, and Bassam Shak'a lost his legs, I was writing a comedy. (About a girl who wouldn't sew the buttons on her husband's jacket.) I hope to maintain myself in comedy. If they blow up any more cars, I'll apprentice myself to a horse-laugh.

≡ ODD MAN

This smoke observer at the dry run for the temple sacrifice phones HQ. Coordinates working out. The bribing smoke goes up, godhead inhales it through a hookah of good will, temple elevation OK, moon dandy. Felicity of doves.

An odd man to belong to a conventicle. Back-slapping and broody. Somewhere between a second-sighted man and a riding master you wouldn't trust with your daughter.

What he phones they note on the smoke-map. Till now, they've justified three hamsters, a budgie confiscated from an atheist's cage, a gecko that might have been the good luck of their house. Now it's doves, the real thing.

Undifferentiated heads bob down there. He could phone anything from his chancy ledge. Prophesy over a dormouse or write a tract. What do they gaping hope for down there? Not to be caught unawares by their temple? Priests, and servants of priests, to be dressed nicely? The table laid?

What if it doesn't, this observer asks himself, the temple doesn't arrive? All that botched linen. Must the shop close down? There's still that matter of Solomon's gold mines. Everyone knows they're located in Mali. By a certain secret correspondence in his gold tooth, he knows where. It whispers him the latitude and longitude of those mines in Mali.

☰ COUTURIER

The clay model of a temple pouts at the side of a sewing machine.

'Can I be intense about my sewing and not about *that?*' says Hanoch. 'I snip back to the First, and forward to the Third, Temple. My cutting is not only religious but chic. My *dernier cri* is heard in the Territories, where young men define themselves. From Ariel to Shilo, they wash out their ears and listen. Yet will they shed their rig-outs? The entire sewing circle of Inner Jerusalem is asking. When will they sink into the archaic mind-set induced by my Josephus tunics?'

'Hanoch,' I say, 'you cannot stop at the chic blessing of a biblical ensemble. We must sink, after all our scurry, into monarchical postures only you can prescribe.' He ponders. He flips through his pattern books. 'A kind of parting of the Red Sea eurhythmics, perhaps?' 'Nothing so harum scarum, Hanoch.' A captain of thousands, poised by a dummy, turns his deliberate head. 'We're relying on you.'

Hanoch takes out of a drawer his sterner designs. Hilltop kings pass out the order of battle. The putting away of magicians. Agag's *First Samuel* haircut. 'Will these do?' I nod. I see fifty thousand, bony and absolute, under the sun of the Lord of Battles. Ponchos cover their simplicity, and in sandals designed by Hanoch they put down their biblical foot where it hurts.

≡ DREAM-TIME

I.

A Judean Orpheus lures back to their stalls a musical herd of leopards and kids and fatlings and cows and bears. They look happily over their half-door at the inspired child.

The Dome of the Rock is hocus pocused away. In the dream-time it flies off—children's building blocks—to Cairo. Aksa, escorted by djinns, lands intact and smiling at Cairo.

A sewing circle of serious young men bend over the vestments of High Priest and Levites. One tries on the mitre of Aaron, the others clap their hands.

On the twenty-sixth floor of a high rise, an exhibition (by invitation only): Palestine earth *circa* 1990.

II.

We vaguely ask them to put up a wall or wash down a car. An intelligent sorcerer casts a slight spell so we don't see them. (Their Farid cigarettes strengthen the smoky feeling.) We attempt an—sometimes we attempt an *Ach-* or a *Hu-* but our syllable falters at a check-point.

☰ FLOWN IN

The helicopter truncheon is a sneak and a bang. It says *He's here, the other one's there.* (Let's hope they sleep out in the fields tonight.)

Concierge-whirr follows us home. We woke up this morning and we'd been mugged too. A dream-truncheon hit us from the Territories.

TRUANTS

Craning toward a Mediterranean milder shore, poets fall
from their balcony. Sheathed in Latin, they do not notice.

Inland, found by the mower, my grasshopper friends cling
to the margin. A crop-eared voice says *Why are you?* They
are shy, it is rough.

ON THE WAY
TO THE TERRITORIES

We're passing a suburb of redemption on the left, the saved like these barrack affairs. They have broody rectangular dreams above which they hang the flag of their disposition.

The more romantic plant Swiss chalets guarded by a bemused militia. Here they yodel a psalm, there they mensurate it in a barrack.

From her twilight hilltop, Brunnhilde mopes at a palisade. A mawkish cement mixer woos a Siegfried moon.

Happiness hides behind the hills. Gun-happiness in holster or from sling or hip. Cowboy.

Under the film-lot moon I ride a horse-laugh: it is not a war-horse unless a laugh is an act of war.

☰ STINGY DUNAMS

I lose my beret down at the farm. I hope the soppy man doesn't pick it up.

After an absence of some years, here he is, mapping not sowing. The owner.

I bend to listen to the land. 'Is he right?' I ask. 'No one owns me,' she says. A grin corrugates her at the doctrine of this poor rustic. A painful horse-laugh leans over the half-door of the stable.

So much for the rustic of this place. Dunces pitchfork me out of this settlement, I run fast as my no doctrine takes me. Foulard de luxe, goodbye.

NOT SETTLING BUT SHUTTLING

They stand under a fig-tree, and giggle. They stick fingers into a prickly pear hedge. Ouch!

What is it? they ask, soppy among wild wheat. Wild what?

I .

ACE

From his hangar of a house, a bird-man emerges. The Captain of Gehenna. With the swagger of a man who's policed the streets from always. Dumbo ears bear him aloft, he circles his barking dunams, then aims his armoured self Hebronwards.

It's a human Flying Fortress. Cartridge belt innards, Kalachnikov, silencer and bowie knife. Face of chewed paper moulded by a puppeteer's worst pupil.

Not so many kilometres off: Spallanzani, attorney bird-man, chest and belly of box-files and wrinkled precedents. Dizzy with diplomas and medals, these airy manikins collide between Jerusalem and Hebron. They bare pinball teeth, grin in recognition, salaam each other on through cumulus land. 'After you, Cap'n.' 'After you, Zap.'

Up there, they've their bird-man's-eye view of subversion. Jehan (Oh temerity!) plants a vine in her backyard. Issa swims crabwise in his pool. Boy Scouts are marching through the streets of Jenin.

They confer in a pepper tree. Back in the capital, they'll caw their info to important legal crows. A shepherd makes a fig at these pedants of the dawn patrol. They flap off, holy and flushed. Then home, and safe, apart from an air current instigated by a sneezing student at An Najah.

The Captain's bundled into his hangar by laughing mechanics. They dust down, clean and oil him, cellophane him all over till the next flight, the next paid-for tirade. Spallanzani's box-filed away, loquacious ace. Here he is, crinkling in his sleep about loops to be looped at the next petty sessions.

2.

EGGWARDS

A new crinkling of paper in the law office at Hebron. *Dr. Spallanzani's with us again.* Secretaries help down Zap from the shelf where he slept off that dawn patrol.

Ears, under cellophane, of the Captain, vibrate in his Gehenna hangar. Struts hum in anticipation of scandal. Ground staff massage the listening posts of his ears. They run a pull-through down his digestive barrels. He's thinking about bombing runs in the Territories, he takes little testing jumps. So it's hard to insert in him a stick of bombs, a medium-sized land mine and combat boots. He wonders about old Zap. Are they spring cleaning him out there in Hebron? Is he glad to be alive in the campaigning season? He'll fly over and check him out.

Spallanzani's helped into his take-off by an overalled Rabbi L★★★. He sniffs buds and subversion everywhere. Secretaries stuff legal papers into gaps in the fuselage. His power of attorney propeller makes them duck, they blow kisses. Zap's off.

II.

The bird-men collide, contrive a recognition, salaam each other on.

'What will it be today, Zap?'

'There's that hen house at Anata.'

'That's true.'

'The eggs there are huge and assertive.'

'That's true.'

'Something else in mind, Cap'n?'

'I'd'

'Say it, Cap'n.'

'challenge any local'

Due to the working of his arms, a recoilless cannon separates itself from the Captain.

'big-eared ace to stand up to me.'

'Fine, even heroic, but'

'Say it, Zap.'

'the eggs at Anata are nationalist.'

III.

The rustle of a living legal library scares the hens. Crowding one end of the coop, they stand on top of each other. Several die. Zap and the Captain scout around. Have they been spotted?

The huge eggs madden the Captain. He takes out his .38 Webley Scott and dispatches them. 'That's for you, Mahmoud, you cockroach.' Working through the coop—he hasn't frequented shooting galleries for nothing—he can hear the Beretta .22 automatic of the Doctor. Egg yolk makes him brave. 'Do you feel, Spallanzani, your Beretta has the right stopping power?'

Zap looks coldly up. 'I'm a bit wary of a Webley Scott. Can a man fulfil his task with a jamming pistol?' The two gunslingers glare at each other above the defeated eggs. They'd rub each other out but women and boys running toward them hint it's time to test the staying power of their wings.

3.

THREE SILLY STRATEGISTS

Militarabbi invites them to the depot.

Hovering above the butts, they exhort the tiros: *Do well.*

They set up target dummies: the Grand Turk and the go-
lem of Prague, Spinoza and the Queen of Heaven, Well-
hausen, Sinbad and the man who made the pyramids.

Cardboard winces and waits.

Watching the trigger-finger whiten, they murmur: *With
G-d's help.*

They waft their wings together, cherubim, above the tab-
ernacle of the butts.

II.

Laughing at militarabbi's showoff field-glasses, they lift
thehim into sky. Eddies of air over Samaria make him
giggly.

Feint here lunge there says this squab but flighty person, and
points at a ridge. *G-d does not believe in feints* snaps Spal-
lanzani. *Sebastia!* cries the Captain, *I'll land there anointed*

and with my knobkerrie. He dashes out the brains of a bird with an unconsidered movement of his favourite accessory. *Yes,* says Spallanzani, *Sebastia's ours for keeps.* Forgotten by the Captain in his enthusiasm, militarabbi topsy-turvies in sky.

Drifted beyond the depot—tiros and flagpoles gone—they look down at straggly Bedouin tents. *I could serve a classic eviction notice,* says Spallanzani. Goats look up at the barmy task-force, on its way to the moon.

Dare you see that nark sitting in the sky? Slumped in a glum old armchair.

Lucky for us he's not looking down. He sticks coloured pins into the map of sky. Zones it. Green has his attention, yellow's next. All cloud will be defined.

Nosy as Pinocchio.

(*Whee oah*. A policevan down here tries three notes of a distraught jelly. Absently he conducts it with his free hand, his working hand tells puce what it is. *Wh-* wags its tail and asks to be stroked.)

Nosy as Pinocchio but deep in magenta.

A new pin.

His brown study is our good luck.

Please, sir, please, mister, please, Your Petulance, don't look down.

☰ VANISHING TRICK

Demographer's defeat: invisibility powder. Rubbed into the skin of a million Ahmeds bused in from the Territories. Into the skin, the hair, the *kefiyeh,* the shirt. For Arabs should be worked but not seen. And not too thrifty with the powder, please. Do you want an Arab button or shirt-sleeve molesting a Jewish street? *Not a sleeve not a sleeve not a sleeve*—that's the new song of the irredentists.

At the building site, a hundred unheld spatulas point the wall. Pails of gravel fill of their own accord.

"The invisibility quotient" (Ministry of Interior) vexes Security but they cope. Jamil the kitchen hand's told to carry a dishcloth, it identifies him; Farrid the plasterer, a trowel. Ahmed's awarded the replica of a dustbin lid.

It's eerie to meet these detached functions filling arteries between Old and New City. Here's a pair of waders asking to be tried on, a thimble works back and forth back and forth, a butcher's cleaver is making its way toward you.

WRECKERS

A nightshift of thieves crowbar out the cornerstone, and slick down a something quarried and cut in the Territories. A hundred grinning men in green berets shore the building up, till the new something is talked into place.

To conclude this event, the untidy sibyl of redemption prophesies in hysterical hexameters.

ON THE HOUSETOPS OF BALATA

The three-day curfew's blanked out a lot but they're up here. Sky's legal, reached by a staircase. Up here, at least a floor higher than the troops.

In this fable by Aesop, men manage to become birds. They salute each other across little parcels of air. 'Space be about you, Marwan.' 'Redoubled space be about you, Raja.'

NOBLE ENCLOSURE

I.

A friend says I've a gnostic squint.

'What do you want me to see?' I say to her. 'It's the Enclosure of a simplifier god I don't much care for. Old *Wahad*. He'd hit a kid with the buckle-end of a belt, he'd do it again, he'd aim the cannon of his very own Sixth Fleet at you and me.'

What does she want me to hear? Is that an ambulance gong, scary across the wadi, or a border guard jeep, racing? I hear a bible attached not to a lectern but to a jeep. Is that the bible jeep? 'Don't you hear it?' I say to her.

II.

So I do what a kid shouldn't. I evict the grumpy father, and fix a place there for the *Matrona* his mother. An apartment for a Latin loan-word. *Matrona*. A tithe-fattened priest won't like that.

I'm looking for her everywhere. Honourable lady a trouble-maker kid never once heard mentioned at the synagogue. It was *Stand still, there in the corner* or *Keep your arms above your head.* (Her moon of thought never stood still.)

Under the stone platform of the Enclosure, she swims around in the *Tehom*. She hangs out there. She'd water the dry god but his agents harry her. He can't bear her liquid pity. She's a loan-word swimming for its life.

Now I don't see her. She can't rest against a side of the *Tehom* because it's not there, and she's not, either. My factory has stopped manufacturing images. (They'll be back, valid and shining.) I can hold on to the rail of this silence perhaps fifteen minutes. No swimming lady or six-shooter god. I'm not a kid in the straw hat and blazer of that time, or today's long-trousered gnostic. To my surprise, I am invisible.

Here we were, under the Temple, and this person said to me *Please hold the matches a moment. I have to do something to this fuse. What d'you have to do to it?* I said. He said *I'm about to blow up the Temple.* Well, really, about to blow up the Temple! I said *Don't do that.*

He stood there and blinked and I saw he knew nothing about fuses. He was a complete butterfingers. Yet you don't buy a fuse if you don't mean to use it. And what are matches for? To be struck.

He said *What d'you come for if you don't want to do it? I'm just tagging along* I said. *Temples are a big thing with me.* He didn't say anything then he said *D'you mind counting how many matches there are in that box? Five* I said. I saw he was thinking about that. He said *They could have put a lot more in that box. They believed in you* I said *they believed five would do.*

He said *What if I asked you to light this fuse?* Well, I've always been very handy. *Go ahead* he said. I lit it. Polite me under the Temple. Which banged.

Pinwheels and rockets should throw light on our cant. Mr. Brock dazzles a Levant sleepyhead.

But it's sluggish sparks, and we've got the vapours.

Speeches!

Twenty two courses of national thought—*Transfer* aperitif, *Transcendence* dessert—young men walking rapidly toward this language.

At night the sparklers.

Now they crank up a Holocaust. We smell a mean gasoline.

Noise travelling up the wadi scoops out a child's bedtime.

Je—(a national soprano tries out the town's name) *ru*—(the baked puff paste of this name ruined the stomachs of many) *sa*—(more died of it than of a napoleon) *sa sa*—(can't travel, stuck in the goo).

Rye—eat a little rye bread for your stomach's sake. Town, here's your rough diet: *Pumper-*
                    nickel   Pumper-
                    nickel   Pumper-
                    nickel the golden
(a flight of Pumpernickels above a gawker's town: a squadron of received notions turns tail and runs).

AMBUSH

I saunter, bow-legged, across duckboards over bad
doctrine.

At queasy street's end, a simplifier eases the Good Book
from his holster. He aims the leaden text for today.

Am I the self-hired sheriff of this town? The star at my
lapcl pales.

ARMOURY
For Wolfgang Yuval

As a hunter cleans his gun so I bend over language.

I picked it from a library shelf, someone must have left it there a long time back.

The muzzle modern and old-fashioned and hard to aim.

Shaky, I cannot aim it. Wolfgang said, *You look like a frightened horse.* I must study in the school of calm.

≡ INDEPENDENCE DAY 1987
≡ *Hospital cake and vaporiser*

Their national flag made its point. Chauvinism bit into the cherry. It was their flagship on my cake.

Clandestine, all night, the vaporiser. It sends a kindly search party of steam and eucalyptus to look down my throat, and tell my inflamed vocal cords to calm down.

I light out on the only unintercepted boat in the Mediterranean. It runs blockades of phlegm.

AMATEUR

We walked with the Old Man of the Mountain through
his secret rooms—teasing a shadow with a scimitar he said
This is for you, Baybars. Today, in the capital, we offer our
back to a provincial without a least knowledge of anatomy.
He must be driving from Jenin with the kitchen knife he's
too stingy to get sharpened beforehand.

PASTORAL

In a greenest European park, an Arab poet throws the cap of a grenade at me. Only the cap but it can kill. He throws it, sadly smiling: I throw it back or kick it back.

An umpire stands at the edge of this tough little dream. He accuses the Arab poet of being an *ironist*. Escaping from irony, I hit him over the head with a rifle-butt. He collapses, he smiles.

SEA MILES

No sooner had I raised my hat in the capital than I found myself chasing it through the marina in Tel Aviv.

It was landlocked felt, passive to the block that formed it, and hadn't learnt to swim.

It was a turncoat hat from piety's suburb.

All the pleasure yachts.

My landlubber hat dips a toe in today, and ponders a famous commentary on blue.

⬛ WATERING PLACE

Sauntering down Prophets' Street—here chunks of thought have solidified and mouldered—I arrive at the street of Antara.

Antara Ibn Shadad. Black knight of the Banu Abs. Mothered by an Abyssinian. Child, therefore, of the Blue Nile.

Sauntering down a received idea—I won't let it conduct me as it has many—I listening bend to Ezekiel's once-subversive waters. His sea, from under the Temple, sniffs the Blue Nile of Antara. It asks to be let out.

Antara tires of uncompromising battle. He sheathes a sword white as his girl's teeth. Dismounts from Abjer his horse. He says he likes this notion of a sea in Ezekiel. He salaams the obdurate man. He says he'll water his horse here.

A sea revives at the words of the great dark figure. It refreshes itself in Nile blue as the eyelids of Abla. Antara ponders. Abjer dips its crescent—'weapon of its brow'— in these waters.

☰ RAFT

Travelling considerable. Huck and Jim—this runaway nig-
ger has handbills printed against him in lynch offices—
Schweik and his Magyar. River holds all: it's the townships
are so ratty.

Schweik snitches for us in the townships. Prague
dogcatcher, Mississippi chickens. He's the batman of the
big river now.

Arkansas Cairo Sidon Tyre. Twenty miles to the free states
(as if we knew where they were).

From the bank a great dark figure on a horse points with
his lance the new direction.

THE RELIEF

In the alternative suburb of the army camp, a young soldier funnels petrol into a command car that will take it 800 kilometres in any direction except up or down.

But a beast is advancing on the Levant in tentacular silence, baffling the simplifiers with the squid-like inkiness of its speculations in the literalist noon.

≡ AFTER THE WAR

All those young men the billiard table
unites, and the poet Saba retrieved in Trieste,
and then there was Schweik and his Magyar friend
at six after the war.

Italian, Slav, Sudeten German,
men from the Alpine countries,

Arab landowner or ex-soldier,
slave, ex-slave, Armenian, Jew, Greek,

from baize or war,
stranded unstingy ones,
generous crossers,
wave at us.

Notes for STINGY KIDS

"Public Transport" *Tzavta:* a Jerusalem theatre. *Hebron:* the centre of Jewish settlement on the West Bank ("the centre of the malignancy", a friend calls it).

" 'The Moonlight Prophet Felt the Madding Hour' " The quotation is from "The Dunciad."

"Neologism" *Abu Tor:* a neighbourhood, part Jewish, part Arab, overlooking Gehenna.

"On the Situation" The cars were blown up by Jewish extremists.

"Odd Man" Solomon's gold mines, it's thought, were located in Mali.

"Couturier" The *Territories:* the West Bank and the Gaza Strip, occupied since 1967. *Ariel* and *Shilo:* Israeli settlements on the West Bank.

"Dream-time" *The Dome of the Rock* and *Aksa:* the Jewish millenarians would like to magic away these Muslim holy places, and replace them with a temple.

59 / D e n n i s · S i l k

"Stingy Dunams" *Dunam:* unit of measure, equal to about one quarter of an acre.

"Ace" *Jenin:* One of the larger Arab towns in the Territories. *An Najah:* an Arab university.

"Eggwards" *Anata:* An Arab village on the West Bank.

"Three Silly Strategists" *Wellhausen:* Julius Wellhausen delved into the composite nature of the *Pentateuch. Sebastia:* Herod the Great enlarged this ancient capital of northern Israel. It's a West Bank village now.

"On the Housetops of Balata" *Balata:* Refugee camp on the outskirts of Nablus.

"Noble Enclosure" A holy place (the Haram As-Sharif) of the Muslims, the Temple Mount of the Jews. *Wahad:* Arabic for *One.* The poem satirizes a literal, and politicized, Muslim and Jewish god. *Tehom:* the primeval depths.

"Amateur" Three Arabs drove in from Jenin and knifed a Jew in the Old City. The Old Man of the Mountain was the head of the Assassins, a medieval order of Muslim fanatics; his enemy, Baybars, was the founder of the Mamluk dynasty.

"Watering Place" *Antara* or *Antar:* a sixth century Arab poet and hero. *Ezekiel's sea:* see Ezek. 47. *Abla:* Antara's girlfriend.

"Raft" and "After the War" I was mistaken about Schweik's friend, who's a Czech and hates Magyars. The mistake seems to work so I've kept it. In James Kirkup's translation, Saba's great poem about Trieste concludes:
> For you bring together the Italian and the Slav,
> Late at night, around your billiard table.

Woyzeck

WOYZECK

Woyzeck watches a big towel pummel a small towel in the scullery. *So that's how it is*, he thinks.

The Captain's left boot gives his right boot a smart kick when it isn't looking. *I'm not to blame for the arrangements*, Woyzeck says to the Captain, who docks his pay for that kick.

☰ THE DOCTOR

I'm a learned man, not like you, Woyzeck. I've been at twelve universities—Bologna and Polonia merely the last of them. It needs patience, I think you'll agree, Woyzeck. I've friends who've taken their first degree after only six universities. I'm not like that, I soldiered on till learning's door opened.

I'm a master of dog Latin. My etymologies bark at the moon. I'm a parasitologist, I've a headful of lice. A good man, yes I'm a good man, Woyzeck.

There you are watering your allotment of peas under the moon. You're my blueprint: a green man. The herds like you.

You're tall under my window, you don't stop growing. That's worrying, Woyzeck. You mutter things to the peas. I aim my eyebrows at you but you don't attend.

You stand there, with scarecrow arms, and expect to fly. You've a primitive notion of flight. Moon-man *circa* 1837. That won't do, Woyzeck. I'll catch you in my cloak, and caw. Eyebrows of the savant will scare your flight.

A Cloud
Inhaled Me

TRUANT

Nights, beside a sleepy young man, I watch my yellow party frock quite irresponsibly cross the big squares of this town. It's Susanna-thin among the town-elders of these buildings. Such stares!

My spook-fist is the knocker at your door. I can't form more of me. My flirts of thought are astral, light.

You're a courtly man, you'd raise duchess fingers to your lips in a doorway of intention. I wish you could. I can't let you have even the X-ray of a fist, old doctor. Yellow is going.

The one who set him up bowls at him
in the alley of the soldiers.
The skiver, the military ninepin,
falls, salutes, focuses
twenty-year-old Astarte among her skittles.

Here Is the Album of Palestine

☰ DREAM CANAAN

And Canaan. How d'you get there?
Easy, in a dream, to get there.
Not boat, or train, or frightening Turk—
with a lump of bread and an apple

down garden, scurry up field,
think through fence and over wall,
I put up my collar because of Jordan chill,
sit down on a sandy hill a bit.

Mounted Ishmaelites snatch off my cap
and chasing I fall into a cellar.
Bottled syrup, soda-jerk Joseph, two
snakes clang cymbals, a blind beggar fiddles.

In circling dream this cellar . . . two saws saw
in desert, over heaped stones, quite near Beit-El.
Wearing a brilliant head scarf and laundered apron,
Mother Rachel gets up to say Hello.

Cooks up millet and honey, brews mead,
slips me, going, pennies to buy cherries with.
Hail stings and clay clings,
will I get out of this alive?

Shadowy spies clutch poles of grape clusters.
A roaring drills the heart, hairs stand up.
This laughing lion'll flick me with his knotted tail.
Open-eyed drowser on a sandy hill.

(*from the Yiddish of Aba Shtoltsenberg*)

≡ AMONG THE SAMARITANS

I .

On the window fronting the street: *Jacob ben Ussi the Samaritan High Priest.* Now isn't that forthcoming? Nothing sneaky, "not a pompous High Priest entering by a secret door."

Refinement, humour, spontaneity and melancholy marked the High Priest. He spoke without much preamble. He was 91 and life had been hard from the start. There'd been that awful World War, he hadn't done much good as the High Priest, so many people to deal with. His grandfather, there, on the wall, he'd been somebody. Anything I needed to ask? One thing he'd say, the Samaritans are the true Israelites. Of course, Gerizim was the authentic temple.

The authentic temple. But it hasn't been there a long time. This notion of a temple *in vacuo,* and that will remain *in vacuo,* is so attractive. I could walk a long cool day around the notion of a temple with such a modest and tremulous High Priest.

Now I asked a silly question. 'You Samaritans are such an old people, don't you get flustered by all these footloose moderns?' He looked at me in alarm. 'No politics,' he said.

II.

The priest Abd-Muin Sadaqa Samari strode through a
pleasant somewhat rooted dream. From the top of Gerizim
he pointed out Hermon ('Up in the North, a long way
off,/ Mount Hermon's got its winter cough,' the Shi'ite
rhyme says). He smiled triumphantly at my surprise.
'Gerizim, is it a good mountain?' 'A very good one,' I said.

The Samaritans hung out under Gerizim. They took a deep
breath before *The Book of Joshua*. Not for us, they said.
And the sulky prophets? Good enough for the Judeans.
Then what about those later talkers? Too many rooms
added by a bumbling architect. Moses' mild five are
enough for us. So they hung on under Gerizim.

They put up their temple here. John Hyrcanus knocked it
down. Then someone put up a pagan temple. Copycat.
Didn't that happen somewhere else? There's altogether too
much doubling in this region. Temples knocked down,
temples put up, two middles of the world (how disorient-
ing), two tombs of Christ. Unity can't take the strain and
forks into duality. Embarrassing.

I liked it up here on Gerizim. It was an airy place with lots
of holes. (They dropped a Byzantine church in this one.)
A high-flying angel spiralled down in the nick of time for
Isaac. Here the priests stand for the slaughter of the Pascal

lambs. We considered the troughs for the slaughter. Poor City of David, it could be dropped, bleating, into one of these troughs.

And Sadaqa Samari had intelligent eyes—Talmudic eyes I'd have said but I don't want to offend him. I asked this friendly man about Samaritan poetry. He himself, he responded, was a poet. He'd written three long poems: one about Moses and Aaron—a *biography*. He tried out this modern word on me, did I know what it meant?—one about secrets, one about names. The names poem was quite special. With his index finger he pointed at sky. Nor was he the only poet among the Samaritans.

Back in his parlour, he offered me liqueur chocolates. Israel's best, he remarked. He'd taken off his priestly outer garment, and discovered an ample burgher-like waistcoat. He showed me the superfluous prophets and a set of Mishna. We don't believe in them but it's important we read them so we can answer back. In his names poem, written out in the patient Arabic of a scribe, he pointed to a passage on the oak at Mamre. Wish I could have read it, Sadaqa Samari.

≡ THE HOLY FIRE

The police captain unfolds his map of the *status quo*. Syrians partitioned off at the Coptic rim, to the west Armenian outworks (and a listening post of Romanian nuns in a recess), a flying column of Greeks outside the Catholicon. Here is Greek security bearing down on Maronite infiltrators.

A pale Frank stands among a wedge of easterners. Her Greek girlfriend must have brought her. Pondering the firehole, a tall Frank in a sun-hat. She's making a foray here. Her friend's glad she brought her, and points out everything.

'The one in the coif there—a bit stuck-up and holy with the attention they're giving her—she's the Sepulchre cleaning lady. That's why she has a place at the tomb door. Brooms and buckets.

'It's the Armenian firehole you're looking at. The Fire Bishop—he's the hero of the day—Damianos is praying hard at the slab over the tomb (that's where the fire starts). Or he's thinking: *My god, I forgot the matches.* Wouldn't that be awful, I mean if he forgot them. Wouldn't he feel a clumsy one, don't you think he'd feel a letter-down of the Greeks? When the fire frisks up to him, he ladles it into this silver bowl he has. He'll be pleased the miracle hasn't kept him waiting. Punctual 1 o'clock. Lucky him! Damianos gathers himself together—after all, he is the Fire Bishop—and hands it out to his helpers. Who hand it out through the firehole. Happy Easter! Damianos comes out. He'll be standing, a little dazed maybe—that's only proper—at the tomb door. The first tapers he lights are the cleaning lady's.' Her Frankish friend laughs. 'But there's a lot of filling-in to do before 1 o'clock.'

Tiya tiya tiya. Syrian piggyback riders. Tarboosh in one hand, hunting crop in the other. A small-town Antar sits akimbo on his friend's back. He's racing in the hippodrome of his lord. From up there, he cries to the Greek chatterbox: 'Who brought this beauty?' Neither answers. The Greek girl rattles on, the tall girl laughs and attends.

☰ THE BOATWOMAN

For a set of etchings by Ivan Schwebel

The demure Latin loan-word *Matrona* (the Lady) was mag-
netized by a thirteenth-century Castilian Cabbalist. He
linked her to the female force in the godhead, whom he
charts in his *Zohar*. He calls her *Matronita*, in his artificial
Aramaic. In Moshe de Leon's thought, she reinforces that
traditional He dying now of loneliness: "He who wishes
to see the King must enter through the holy city . . . Every
message to the King is sent through the Matrona—every
message from the lower spheres to the King must first
reach the Matrona. From her it goes to the King." (*Zohar,
Beshalach*)

Moshe de Leon calls her also *Jerusalem*. It is clear she is
more than a sky-thought, she must be the daily Jerusalem
we walk through. As in the old rhyme:

> Heavens above, heavens below,
> Stars above, stars below,
> All that is over, under doth show,
> Happy thou who the riddle readest.

For if she's not here, she's not there. If she's not there,
she's not here. We have to think ourselves double, a friend
said. We have to think her double.

Moshe de Leon calls her also *Sea*. Then she's in the town-water. She's in the tumbler we drink from, the water we wash in. We have to think her double, we have to wash ourselves double. Hard work!

Moshe de Leon calls her also the *Shechinah* (the indwelling). Better the *Shechanah* (the neighbour) than the *Shechinah*, said another friend. The answer is, she's both. She's hard to sort out.

In Ivan Schwebel's etchings, she's a brisk young woman-lawyer hurrying down Ben Yehuda Street, and instead of papers she carries the town-plan. Or she's a full-skirted thought hovering over Mamilla Street. Or she punts along the margin of Kiryat Yovel, and contrives a little brook to water that dry botched suburb.

This loan-word is a woman asking much of us. Ivan Schwebel has answered her with a system of moody canals that criss-cross and surprise Jerusalem.

IN MEMORIAM
After Ungaretti

He was named
Mohammed Sceab

descendant
of emirs of nomads

suicide
because he had no country

loved France
and changed his name
was Marcel
and never French

no longer knew
cushions of his own tent
where, sipping coffee,
they listen to a singsong Koran

didn't know
to free
the song
of his dispersion

I together
with the hotel proprietress
of number five rue des Carmes Paris
accompanied
him down a descending alley

he lies
in the cemetery
at Ivry

suburb with its persistent look
of a departing fair

maybe I
alone know
that he lived

≡ BOOK OF HOURS

Summer the Semite
among hills.
Winter the Flemish man
and his glum dog.

JAFFA GATE

Cack-handed man
topsy-turvy column

Base says to sky *Don't blame me*
shaft sends back its worries to capital
the skivvy of earth down there

And this whole colonnade is logical
and you are, too,
and stride through it on your hands.

☰ A MISUNDERSTANDING

An old teacher married a handsome girl. He bought a duck one day, it was his favourite dish, and sent it home for her to roast.

Her lover, arriving first, ate the duck.

But when the old man returned, she said she'd never seen it. She denied that duck.

He bought a second duck and carried it home himself. Again her lover ate it. The poor husband was left to digest the matter.

The third time, the teacher took his students with him to the poulterer, bought a third duck, and the students saw him back with it. He invited a guest to the third meal. To see what happened.

Of course, again the wife had cooked her lover the duck. How would she get out of her scrape?

She said to her husband to run out and buy a lettuce and salt. Alone with his guest, she hummed and sharpened a carving knife. He asked what she was doing. 'My husband

can't afford duck,' she said. 'The truth is, he's schizo-
phrenic. He thinks his guests are ducks, he likes carving
them up. I think you should respect but not trust him. I'd
say you should make off while you can.'

The old man bringing back the salt and lettuce, his wife
cried, 'Hey hey hey! your friend's run off with the duck.
Run after him, maybe you can cut off a piece of your duck.
Here's the knife.'

Knife in hand, the husband ran after his bolting guest.
'Hey hey hey!' he cried, 'won't you stop? Just a piece, just
a piece, a little piece.'

'No no no,' the bolting guest cried, 'not a little, not a
single piece.'

Teacher and friend lost a delicious meal.

(*Passed on by Mr. George Kaplanian, whose source was an Arab
from Ramallah.*)

DO IT YOURSELF
The Overland Route

window-wiper
cartridge
sniper.
umbrage.

change tire?
can't.
Sidon and Tyre.
cant!

car-key
kerb.
khaki
curb.

,Tripoli,
unhappily.

What the Spies Said to Moses

bad vibes
tribes
Palestine
Frankenstein.

PERFORMANCES

Actor poor-box
slit for sky-coin.

And in '67
manhandling that searchlight
to be trained on the enemy.

Someone phones the cue
to the roof position.

1948

The first battles bore
scary love-flowers
with almost-finishing kisses like shells.
Boy-soldiers in our elegant town-buses—
number 12 number 8 number 5—
drive to the front.

(*From the Hebrew of Yehuda Amichai*)

CHRISTMAS

I.

Town is a terrible meander.

They pay off the taxi and get out.

George memory among the Armenians Kaplanian.
Gabriel, from Abyssinia the black one.
Dennis of Jewry.

The three Magi descend on the Church of Mary Magdalen
bearing the spices of themselves
but a surly prioress puts down the black one.
Only the Arab novice rolling unrolling the carpet wants
    to enfold him in it.

I I.

We had been walking through the artichoke heart of town
which should be eaten, leaf by leaf, in the afternoon,
but a mean fungoid
ate it.

To be provincial is death so my lines are metropolitan.
I don't want to meander.

Eating Out

☰ EATING OUT

We're eating out with the rich, Vallejo and me. They at-
tend, almost respectful, to his forehead, and to the hand-
kerchief even a poorest Peruvian flies from his breast
pocket. I'm his posthumous secretary, I write down what
he says among the messes of the rich. He does his best to
rescue the meal from chronic poorness that gets into the
oven, into the flour, into the curlicue on the plate, into
the cruet of oil. The dishes are a deputation that lost its
way. Embarrassed, he talks of other things, is hard on me
for overuse of *I you we she*. Give more time to *it,* and the
they in *it,* he says. Next time, he says, let's eat in the
kitchen.

≡ THINKING ABOUT GABRIEL

I said to the old poet
I want to belong to your entourage
(a frail schoolboy, he waited for his hotel-bill)
and he said *Do you want to be a count*
or a baronet?
                    I settled for a baronet
and knelt for his accolade
(he was leaving for New York at A.M.
because he needed a change of parish)
but it wasn't a ponderous *Sir,*
no, he gave me the kiss of the guest, going.

LUCKY STRIKE

Singeing through my Dante a cigarette
(only accident in a conscious poem?)
hurries the purgation of tardy Belacqua.

AERIAL DAYS
Ivan Schwebel's Zion Square drawings

Crummy stairs
climbed, you lean
and look. Balcony
years your good pencil
waited. The patient
need you.

Does he really
climb? the Kapulski
lounging brothers
at their tall till
ask. *Will he give back*
pastry-cook white?

Town and a cake
wait.
      The cinema
queue dies, animal.
Last show at flicks.
Light, Ivan, that hall
the usher thought dark.

☰ UPTOWN

I.

Barber 82 Street–Broadway

An enthusiast
harrowed the curly ridges with a hairbrush
but his soft cut brought out the fullness.

I liked his careful snipping.

He understood my eyebrows, conceded
they're a good pair and not to be toyed with.

I I.

You got me wrong

This tenant, thinking me the landlord's man,
locks the bathroom door on green me.
He says I've given trouble to his mother
long enough. Here's me, him and wall.

It's hard, quite hard, to persuade him that
I'm only up here in 2D to inquire
about the leak in the 1D ceiling.

99 / D e n n i s · S i l k

MILLAMANT TO MIRABELL
(Variation on Melanie's "I Wish I Were a Farmer")

Footpads in silk
that steal our breath, Fain-
alls, a London
I'll not like:—

take me away
to that knifethin mountain air
and I will pick an apple
that isn't there.

PRESIDENTIAL ELECTIONS

STRATEGIES OF
AMERICAN ELECTORAL POLITICS

PRESIDENTIAL ELECTIONS

Strategies of American Electoral Politics

NELSON W. POLSBY

Wesleyan University

AARON B. WILDAVSKY

University of California, Berkeley

CHARLES SCRIBNER'S SONS, *New York*

For Linda and Carol

PREFACE

THIS book has had a long, and for us a very happy, gestation. Each of us has had over the last decade a chance to watch from a distance several Presidential elections; we have from time to time examined the scholarly literature on the subject, collected data on our own, and tried to think systematically about them independently of one another. In the winter of 1956-57, while we were graduate students at Yale, our collaboration began, with an effort at disentangling the theoretical and practical implications of then current proposals for party reform. Since then, we have repeatedly returned to American electoral politics in conversation and in our thoughts and writing. Despite considerable differences in the ways in which we express ourselves, and occasional differences in the emphases we would give to different events, we have been able to arrive at agreement on virtually all of the issues raised in this book. It is a totally collaborative effort in that we ourselves would have difficulty tracing the genesis or development of ideas contained here to one of us or the other.

Along the way, we have incurred many intellectual debts, separately and jointly. Some of our obligations are mentioned in the footnotes, but others, of a more personal kind, should be noted here. Nelson W. Polsby wants especially to thank Malcolm C. Moos, Harvey Wheeler, and Ralph M. Goldman, who originally got him interested in Presidential election politics, and who helped to guide his first preliminary researches into the decision-making of the Democratic National Convention of 1952. Robert A. Dahl stimulated an approach to political analysis that led to a paper describing the logic of national convention behavior. This paper appeared as "Decision-Making at the National Conventions," *Western Political Quarterly* 13 (September 1960), 609-619. Lewis A. Froman, Jr., collaborated with him on a paper which served as forerunner and prototype of the treatment in this volume of the Electoral College. He also received excellent assistance from Margaret MacGregor Spellman, Carolyn Stoakes, Sheila Jones, and Martha Leiserson, who typed several versions of our manuscript, and from Bruce Franklin, Paul D. O'Brien, John R. Hanson, Peter Fritts, Charles L. Zetterberg, and Michael Austin, who ran down footnotes, read proof, and performed other odious chores cheerfully and well. Much of this work was made possible by a Ford Foundation Grant to Wesleyan University.

Aaron Wildavsky wants to thank the students in his senior seminar at Oberlin College for their stimulating discussion and for the preparation of a series of papers on past national conventions. He is grateful to the Eagleton Institute of Politics for a National Convention Fellowship which enabled him to study the behavior of the Ohio delegation at the 1960 Democratic Convention. The results of this enterprise were published as " 'What Can I Do?': Ohio Delegates View the Convention," in Paul Tillet, ed., *Inside Politics: The National Conventions, 1960* (Dobbs Ferry, N. Y., 1962). While at the convention, he benefited from conversations with James D. Barber.

Together, we are grateful for the lasting inspiration and repeated encouragement of our teachers, David B. Truman and Allan P. Sindler, and, for excellent critical readings of earlier versions of this work, to Richard F. Fenno, Fred I. Greenstein, Lewis A. Froman, Jr., H. Douglas Price, Milton C. Cummings, Jr., Michael Leiserson, Duane Lockard, Allan P. Sindler, Herbert E. Alexander, Elmer E. Cornwell, and Paul G. Willis.

It is customary for joint authors each to receive half the credit for their work, but to be blamed for all its errors. In this instance, as, we are sure, in so many, the credit deserves to be even more widely dispersed. We need hardly volunteer to our readers information about the sources of error.

N.W.P.

A.B.W.

July, 1963
Washington, D.C.

CONTENTS

PREFACE   vii

INTRODUCTION: Political Strategies and Presidential

        Elections   1

CHAPTER

ONE *THE STRATEGIC ENVIRONMENT*   5

Voters
Interest Groups and Voting Blocs
Parties
The Electoral College
The Distribution of Resources
 Money
 Control Over Information
 The Presidency
 Convertability of Resources
Summary

TWO *THE NOMINATING PROCESS*   59

Strategic Considerations
 Goals
 Uncertainty
 Power
Pre-Convention Strategies
 Primaries
 State and District Conventions
At the Convention
 What the Participants Are Doing
 Candidates and Their Organizations
 Delegates
 Straws in the Wind
 The Balloting
 The Vice-Presidential Nominee
Appendix: Selection of Delegates to National Conventions

THREE *THE CAMPAIGN*   102

Theory and Action
Ins and Outs
Friends, Volunteers, and Professionals
Where to Campaign?

xi

CHAPTER

    Party Identification
    Domestic Issues
    Foreign Affairs
    Presentation of Self
    The Television Debates
    Getting a Good Press
    Mud-Slinging
    Feedback
    Appendix: Predicting Elections

FOUR   *REFORM?*   143

    The Political Theory of Party Reform
    The Bias Behind Party Reform
    Is Broad-Gauged Party Reform Possible?
    Is Broad-Gauged Party Reform Desirable?
      An Appraisal of the Nomination Process
    Is Broad-Gauged Party Reform Desirable?
      An Appraisal of the Electoral College
    Is Broad-Gauged Party Reform Desirable?
      Party Differences and Political Stability
    Is Party Reform Relevant?

FIVE   *THE BALLOT AND THE POLITICAL SYSTEM*   189

    Coalitions in the System
    Elections and Public Policy
    Extremism
    Party Competition and Policy

APPENDIX A   207

    1964 Presidential Primaries

APPENDIX B   209

    Convention Delegates and the Electoral College,
      1960 and 1964

BIBLIOGRAPHY   211

INDEX   213